Bees

There wouldn't be sunflowers,
Wouldn't be peas,
Wouldn't be apples
On apple trees,
If it weren't for fuzzy old,
Buzzy old bees
Dusting pollen
From off their knees.

— Aileen Fisher

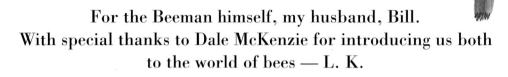

For the Beeman himself, my husband, Bill.
With special thanks to Dale McKenzie for introducing us both
to the world of bees — L. K.

A mis pequeñas abejitas, Facundo y Olivia — V. C.

The publisher would like to thank Dr Dewey M. Caron, Professor of Entomology and Wildlife
Ecology at the University of Delaware, for lending his academic expertise to this project; and
Chris Deaves, Chair of the Education and Husbandry sub-committee, British Beekeepers' Association,
for his assistance with this project.

Barefoot Books
2067 Massachusetts Ave
Cambridge, MA 02140

Barefoot Books
294 Banbury Road
Oxford, OX2 7ED

Text copyright © 2008 by Laurie Krebs. Illustrations copyright © 2008 by Valeria Cis
The moral rights of Laurie Krebs and Valeria Cis have been asserted

First published in Great Britain by Barefoot Books, Ltd and in the United States of America by Barefoot Books, Inc in 2008
The paperback edition first published in 2009
All rights reserved

Graphic design by Judy Linard, London
Reproduction by Bright Arts, Singapore
Printed in China on 100% acid-free paper
This book was typeset in Thoughts 39 point and Bodoni 28 on 42 point
The illustrations were prepared in acrylics on paper

ISBN 978-1-84686-260-1

British Cataloguing-in-Publication Data: a catalogue record for this book is available from the British Library

Library of Congress Cataloging-in-Publication Data is available under LCCN 2007025060

3 5 7 9 8 6 4

"Apple and Honey Muffins" from *The Honey Kitchen Cookbook*, reprinted by kind permission of Dadant & Sons, Inc.

The Beeman

Written by Laurie Krebs

Illustrated by Valeria Cis

Barefoot Books
Step inside a story

Here is my Grandpa, who's known in our town as the **Beeman**.

Here is his **jacket**,
with zipped-up hood,
that covers his face
just the way that it should
when he visits his hives
as the Beeman.

Here are his **gloves**, made of cotton and leather, protecting his hands in all kinds of weather when he tends to his hives as the Beeman.

Here is the **beehive**, where all the bees sleep, tucked into a box called a **shallow** or **deep** and then placed on a stand by the Beeman.

Here is the **smoker**,
that calms down the bees,
and a **hive tool** that opens
the beehive with ease
for a much closer look
by the Beeman.

Here is the **queen bee**,
who does her job well,
and lays tiny eggs
in a six-sided cell.
"She's the heart of the hive,"
says the Beeman.

Here are the **drone bees**,
with big bulging eyes,
and a large appetite
supporting their size.
"They mate with the queen,"
adds the Beeman.

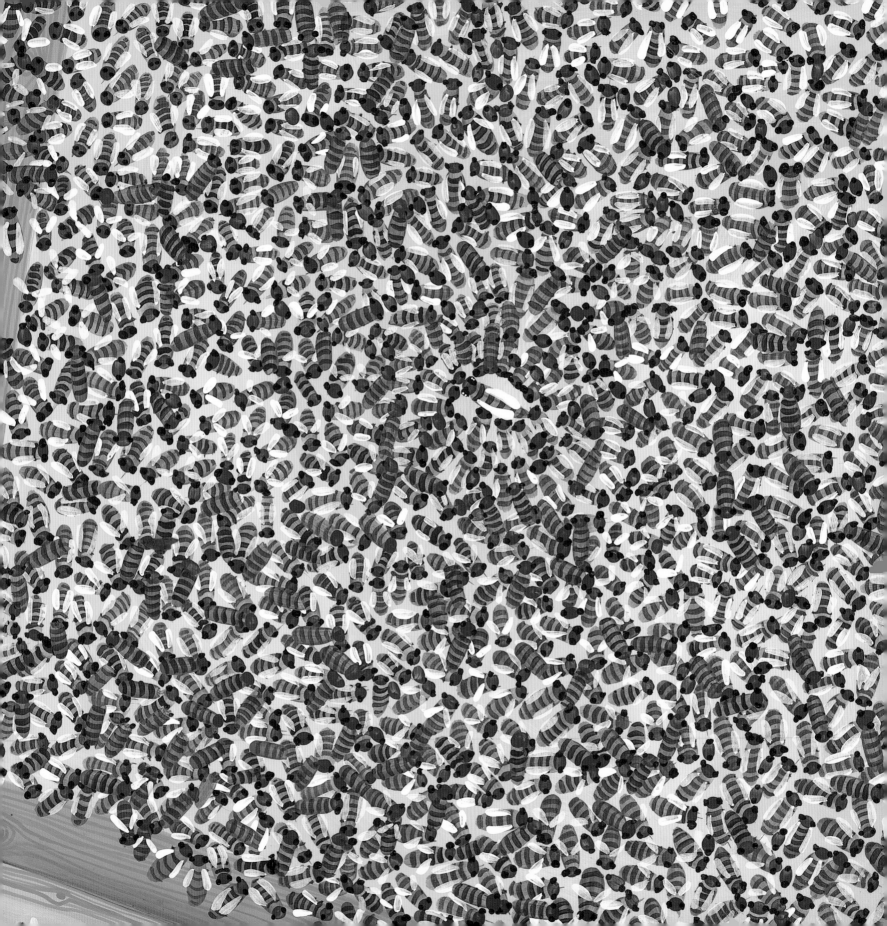

Here are the **workers**,
ten thousand or more,
who gather the **nectar**
to bring back and store
in **honeycomb cells**
for the Beeman.

Here are the **house bees** with swift-moving wings, that dry up the **nectar** a worker bee brings, making honey for me and the Beeman.

Here's the **extractor**,
its "clickety-clack"
removing the **honey**
from **frames** on its rack
and filling up jars
for the Beeman.

Here's some of the **honey**,
returned to the hive.
It's food for the bees
to help them survive
the long winter days
near the Beeman.

Here are the **bees**,
protected from harm,
inside the **hive**
huddled snug and warm.
"So they'll be here next year,"
says the Beeman.

Here is the wagon,
filled up to the brim,
with bottles of **honey**
collected by him
and brought to the house
by the Beeman.

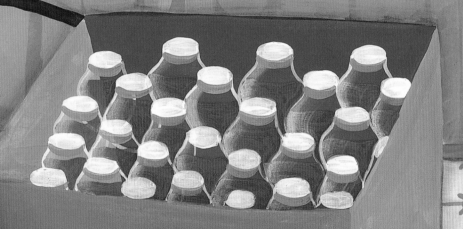
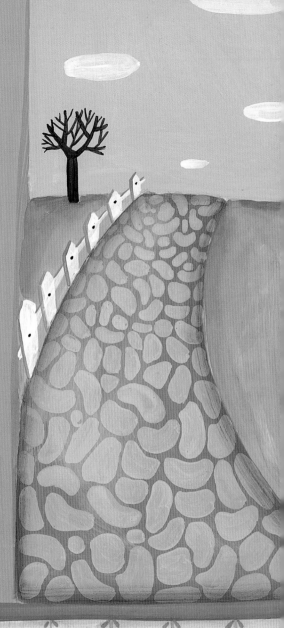

Here are the **muffins**,
all warm and delicious,
and dripping with **honey**
on Grandma's best dishes.

I'm glad that my Grandpa's
the Beeman.

Bees

Bees belong to the insect family. They have six legs, three body parts (head, thorax and abdomen), two pairs of wings, two antennae and two compound eyes that let them see in all directions.

A bee begins as an *egg* placed in a tiny cell by the queen. The egg hatches into a worm-like creature called a *larva*. The larva changes to a *pupa*, and hidden inside the tiny cell, the pupa turns into a *bee*. When it hatches, the bee is fully grown and ready to be a member of the colony. It takes about three weeks to go from an egg to a bee.

Bee Colonies

Bees live in large groups called *colonies*. A colony of bees has one queen, several hundred drones and tens of thousands of workers.

Drone bees are male bees. They have huge black eyes and plump bodies. They don't work inside the hive or collect nectar and pollen. They mate with the queen.

The *queen bee* has a slender body and is longer than the other bees. She is also the mother of them all. Her job is to lay eggs. In spring's busy season, she lays between one and two thousand eggs every day.

Worker bees are female and they have many different jobs. Sometimes they feed the larvae and tidy up the hive. Or they create wax and use it to make new cells. Sometimes they groom the queen and give her a rich protein food called *royal jelly*. Or they protect the hive from enemies by standing guard at the entrance. Sometimes they leave the hive to gather nectar, pollen or water. Their jobs depend on what the colony needs them to do.

Beekeeping

Diseases and pests have killed most of the wild bees, so today, beekeepers take care of the colonies. They provide weatherproof boxes where bees live. They act as insect doctors and supply medicine to keep the colony healthy. They check the queen to see that she is strong and that new bees are developing.

Just before autumn, the beekeepers harvest the hives' extra honey, making sure they put back enough honey for the bees to use all winter. Beekeepers have special clothing that helps them do their job safely. They wear long gloves, coveralls, boots and a hood with a protective veil to keep away curious bees.

Hives

A beekeeper's *hives* are the boxes where the colony lives, raises its young and stores its honey and pollen. Large wooden boxes called deeps are placed on the bottom. Stacked on top of the deeps are shallows, smaller boxes that hold the honey. As they are filled, more shallows are added by the beekeeper and the tower grows taller.

Frames and Honeycomb Cells

Frames are man-made wooden rectangles that support the honeycomb. They are lined up in the shallows and deeps like folders in a filing cabinet. The *honey-comb* is the cluster of wax cells built onto the frames by the bees to hold eggs, larvae, pupae, honey or pollen.

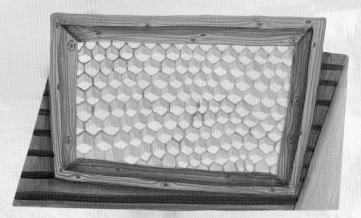

Smoker

Beekeepers use a metal container called a *smoker*, in which they build a smoky fire. When beekeepers inspect the hive, they puff the smoke to calm the bees.

Hive tool

A *hive tool* is used to help the beekeeper pry open the hive to examine it.

Extractor

When it's time to harvest the honey, beekeepers remove the frames from the shallows. With a hot knife, they cut away the wax cappings from the cells and place the frames inside a large bin called an *extractor*. It spins the frames, and honey splashes against the walls, collecting at the bottom of the bin. Beekeepers open the extractor's spigot and fill their jars with the tasty liquid.

About Honey

Honey tastes delicious! People have enjoyed it for thousands of years. At first, it was gathered from the nests of wild bees. Later, people made hives of clay or straw and kept bees (and the honey they made) near their homes.

Honey begins as *nectar*, the sweet watery juice inside a flower blossom. A worker bee unrolls her long tongue, called a *proboscis*, and sucks up the liquid, just as though she were using a straw. Back in the hive, other workers put the nectar into cells and fan it to drive out the moisture. After many trips to the flowers and lots of fanning, the nectar juice thickens into honey. When the honey is ripe, the bees cap the cell with wax to keep it fresh.

Pollination

Bees are important insects. Without them, we wouldn't have many delicious fruits, nuts and vegetables.

As bees travel to find nectar, they brush past the part of the flower that holds powder-like grains called pollen. The pollen clings to their hairy bodies. When they move on to visit the next blossom, some of this pollen is left on the seed-making part of that flower. Because of this, in time, fruits, nuts and vegetables will grow. Bees help by carrying the pollen from one flower to another, allowing the process of pollination to occur.

Bee Dancing

Did you know that bees dance? Well, they do, and their dance tells other workers where nectar is found and how to get there. If food is close by, they do a *round dance*, running in circles, first one way and then the other, allowing the workers to smell and taste what they have found. The faster they dance, the richer the supply of nectar.

If food is further from the hive, they do a *wagtail dance*. The longer they waggle, the longer the trip will be. Making a half circle in one direction, they turn sharply and waggle in a straight line, until they again turn sharply and make a half circle in the opposite direction. The orientation of the dancer inside the hive tells the workers the direction in which they should fly.

Grandma's Apple and Honey Muffins

220g or 2 cups sifted flour

3 tsp baking powder

1 tsp salt

$\frac{1}{2}$ tsp cinnamon

$\frac{1}{4}$ tsp nutmeg

80g or 1 cup whole wheat or bran cereal flakes

20g or $\frac{1}{4}$ cup finely chopped walnuts (optional)

40g or $\frac{1}{2}$ cup raisins

100g or 1 cup grated apple

2 eggs

160ml or $\frac{2}{3}$ cup honey

120ml or $\frac{1}{2}$ cup milk

4 tbsp or $\frac{1}{4}$ cup vegetable oil

Sift flour with baking powder, salt and spices. Add cereal, walnuts, raisins and apple. Beat eggs well; add honey, milk and oil. Add liquid mixture all at once to flour mixture, stirring just to blend. Grease muffin cups and fill $\frac{2}{3}$ full. Bake at 200°C/400°F for 18–20 minutes.

Makes 18 muffins.